Nana IN THE City

BY LAUREN CASTILLO

CLARION BOOKS

Houghton Mifflin Harcourt

Boston • New York

Clarion Books • 215 Park Avenue South, New York, New York 10003 • Copyright © 2014 by Lauren Castillo
All rights reserved. • For information about permission to reproduce selections from this book, write to Permissions,
Houghton Mifflin Harcourt Publishing Company, 215 Park Avenue South, New York, New York 10003.
Clarion Books is an imprint of Houghton Mifflin Harcourt Publishing Company. • www.hmhco.com
The illustrations were executed in watercolors. • The text was set in 23-point Powhatten.
Library of Congress Cataloging-in-Publication Data • Castillo, Lauren, author, illustrator.
Nana in the city / by Lauren Castillo. • pages cm • Summary: A young boy is frightened
by how busy and noisy the city is when he goes there to visit his Nana, but she makes him a fancy
red cape that keeps him from being scared as she shows him how wonderful a place it is.
ISBN 978-0-544-10443-3 (hardcover) • [1. City and town life—Fiction.
2. Grandmothers—Fiction. 3. Courage—Fiction.] I. Title.
PZ7.C2687244Nan 2014 • [E]—dc23 • 2013043953
Manufactured in the USA • PHX 10 9 8 7 6 5 4 3
4500525460

For Nannie, Frances, Great-Aunt Virginia,
and city-livin' nanas everywhere

I went to stay with Nana at her new apartment in the city.

I love my nana,

but I don't love the city.

The city is busy.

The city is loud.

The city is filled with scary things.

It is no place for a nana to live.

But Nana says the city is wonderful—

bustling,

booming,

and extraordinary.

She says it is the perfect place for a nana to live.

At night, the room rumbles and shakes.

There is no sleeping here. . . .

"Nana, aren't you afraid in the city?
It is busy, loud, and filled with scary things."

Nana gave me a kiss.
Tucked my blanket in nice and tight.
"Tomorrow," she said, "I will show you how
wonderful the city is."

When I woke up in the morning, Nana was holding
a fancy red cape.

"For you to wear on our walk today," she said.
"You'll see that the city is not scary at all."

I felt

brave

in my cape.

We got ready and left the apartment.

The city was busy.

The city was loud.

But Nana was right. The city
was not filled with scary things....

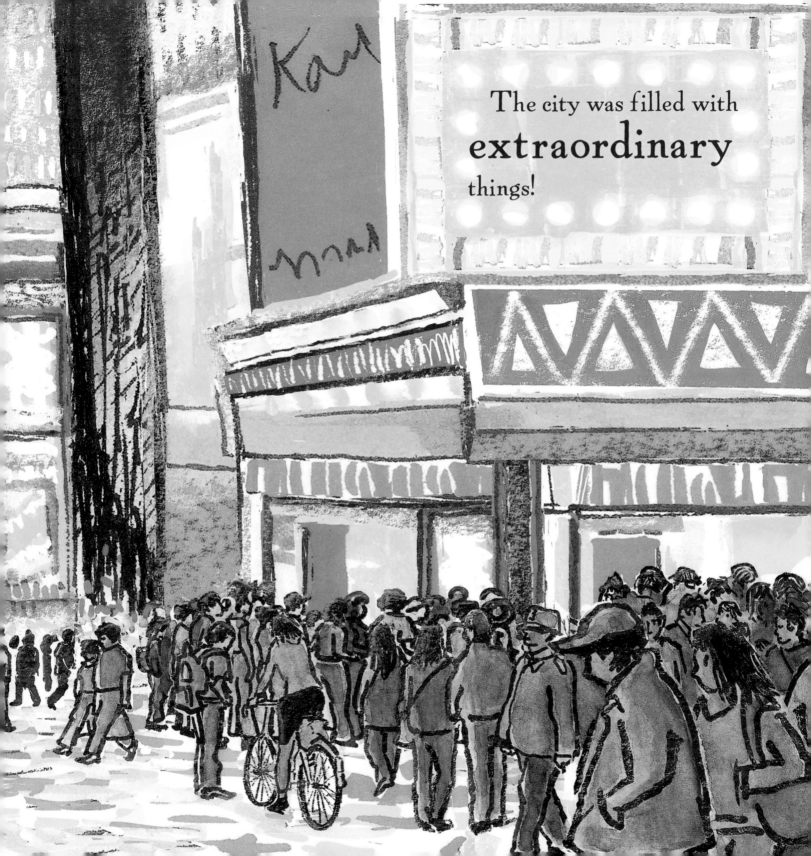

The city was filled with **extraordinary** things!

There is so much for a nana to do in this city!

When it was time to leave, I wrapped Nana in my cape.
"This will keep you brave," I tell her.

The city is busy, the city is loud, and it is the
absolute perfect place for a nana to live.

And for me to visit!